MAY 2017

Kay's Maze Phase

Anders Hanson

Consulting Editor, Diane Craig, M.A./Reading Specialist

ABDO
Publishing Company

Published by ABDO Publishing Company, 4940 Viking Drive, Edina, Minnesota 55435.

Printed in the United States.

Credits
Edited by: Pam Price
Curriculum Coordinator: Nancy Tuminelly
Cover and Interior Design and Production: Mighty Media
Photo and Illustration Credits: BananaStock Ltd., Brand X Pictures, Comstock, Digital Vision, Eyewire Images, Anders Hanson, Hemera, Image 100, PhotoDisc, Rubberball Productions

Library of Congress Cataloging-in-Publication Data

Hanson, Anders, 1980-
    Kay's maze phase / Anders Hanson.
       p. cm. -- (Rhyme time)
    ISBN 1-59197-798-3 (hardcover)
    ISBN 1-59197-904-8 (paperback)
    1. English language--Rhyme--Juvenile literature. I. Title. II. Rhyme time (ABDO Publishing Company)

PE1517.H3755 2004
428.1'3--dc22
                                                                    2004047365

SandCastle™ books are created by a professional team of educators, reading specialists, and content developers around five essential components that include phonemic awareness, phonics, vocabulary, text comprehension, and fluency. All books are written, reviewed, and leveled for guided reading, early intervention reading, and Accelerated Reader® programs and designed for use in shared, guided, and independent reading and writing activities to support a balanced approach to literacy instruction.

Let Us Know

After reading the book, SandCastle would like you to tell us your stories about reading. What is your favorite page? Was there something hard that you needed help with? Share the ups and downs of learning to read. We want to hear from you! To get posted on the ABDO Publishing Company Web site, send us e-mail at:

sandcastle@abdopub.com

SandCastle Level: Fluent

Words that rhyme do not have to be spelled the same. These words rhyme with each other:

ballets

hoorays

blaze

maze

days

phase

essays

praise

glaze

ways

Darcy wears a pretty costume
when she dances in **ballets**.

Andy's family went on a winter vacation.

They stayed for five **days**.

Sam and Ilene's horse is named Orion.

He has a white **blaze** on his nose.

Donnie's soccer team won the trophy.

They all shout loud **hoorays**!

Ina works on her paper.

She likes writing **essays**.

Mitch uses a telescope to learn about each **phase** of the moon.

Kenny looks through the holes in the doughnuts.

His face gets covered with **glaze**.

Regina is a good reader.

Her teacher gives her lots of praise.

Patty follows Jason through a hedge maze.

Emily's class is learning to use computers in many different **ways**.

Kay's Maze Phase

Kay didn't know how to spend her days.

She wasn't interested in writing essays

or practicing ballets.

Kay's father said, "It's only a phase.
She can't spend every day in her PJs."

One day Kay saw a sign with the phrase, "Fastest one through the maze wins a donut with cherry glaze."

Kay spent days upon days
learning maze after maze.

When Kay tried a practice maze,
she did it with no delays.

Kay's friends gave her lots of praise.

On race day, Kay ran through the maze in a blaze.

Her parents were so proud, they shouted hoorays!

Hooray! Hooray!

Rhyming Riddle

What do you call compliments on frosting?

Glaze praise

Glossary

blaze. a white or light-colored stripe or spot on an animal's face; to go extremely fast

essay. a short paper about a single subject

hedge. a fence or wall made by planting shrubs or small trees very close together

maze. an intricate, confusing network of connected paths that you try to find your way through

phase. a stage of the moon's changing appearance as it travels around the Earth; a temporary interest, mood, or pattern of behavior

telescope. a magnifying device used to look at things that are very far away

About SandCastle™

A professional team of educators, reading specialists, and content developers created the SandCastle™ series to support young readers as they develop reading skills and strategies and increase their general knowledge. The SandCastle™ series has four levels that correspond to early literacy development in young children. The levels are provided to help teachers and parents select the appropriate books for young readers.

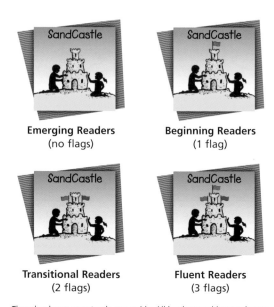

Emerging Readers
(no flags)

Beginning Readers
(1 flag)

Transitional Readers
(2 flags)

Fluent Readers
(3 flags)

These levels are meant only as a guide. All levels are subject to change.

To see a complete list of SandCastle™ books and other nonfiction titles from ABDO Publishing Company, visit www.abdopub.com or contact us at:
4940 Viking Drive, Edina, Minnesota 55435 • 1-800-800-1312 • fax: 1-952-831-1632